THIS BLOOMSBURY BOOK

BELONGS TO

....

To my family
and the river gypsies

First published in Great Britain in 2003 by Bloomsbury Publishing Plc
36 Soho Square, London, W1D 3QY
This paperback edition with CD first published in 2006

Audio CD recorded and produced at the Showreel
Read by Jonny Magnanti, with original music by Touchwood Media
Copyright in recording © and ℗ Bloomsbury Publishing 2006

A CIP catalogue record of this book is available from the British Library
ISBN 0 7475 8873 2
ISBN-13 9780747588733

Colour separation by Bright Arts Graphics, Singapore
Printed in Singapore by Tien Wah Press

1 3 5 7 9 10 8 6 4 2

Marvin Wanted MORE!

Joseph Theobald

BLOOMSBURY
CHILDREN'S
BOOKS

The sheep in the meadow loved
to play together all day long.

But Marvin was feeling rather gloomy.

"What's the matter?" asked Molly.

"I can't run as fast or jump as high as the other sheep," grumbled Marvin. "I'm too small, it's not fair."

"But I like you as you are," said Molly.

But Marvin wanted to be just a little bigger.
So when the other sheep had finished eating…

...Marvin ate some more.

As Marvin ate more,
he grew bigger
and bigger...

And soon he could run faster and jump much higher than the other sheep.

But as he grew bigger and bigger
he just wanted more **and more...**

...until he could not stop!

"Don't eat the forest!" called the other sheep.
"You're getting too big!" cried Molly.

But Marvin loved being bigger.
"Just a **little bit more**," he said.

And he munched up the forest in a matter of minutes!
"That's enough!" shouted Molly.
But Marvin was too busy to listen.

He gobbled up mountains and...

drank whole lakes. But Marvin still wanted **more**...

Then he swallowed an entire country in one big gulp!
But Marvin still wanted just a little bit more...

So he jumped
onto the moon...

and ate the world!

But then Marvin stopped. He was all alone.
He missed the trees, and the meadow, and
the other sheep, but most of all he missed Molly.
And this made him feel very, very ill.

Then all of a sudden...

Marvin was sick.
Out came the world and everything with it.

Although things weren't quite the same
as they were before...

Marvin felt much better.

"I like you just the way you are," whispered Molly.

"I like me just the way I am, too," said Marvin.

Enjoy more great picture books from Bloomsbury ...

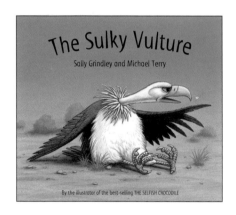

The Sulky Vulture

Sally Grindley & Michael Terry

Busy Night

Ross Collins

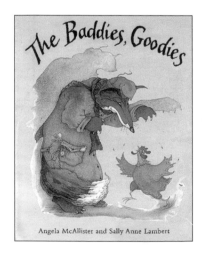

The Baddies' Goodies

Angela McAllister & Sally Anne Lambert

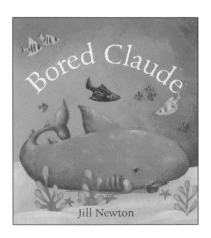

Bored Claude

Jill Newton